When it's hard to
breathe

Judith Condon

W
FRANKLIN WATTS
LONDON • SYDNEY

This edition published in 2002 by Franklin Watts,
96 Leonard Street, London EC2A 4XD

Franklin Watts Australia,
56 O'Riordan Street,
Alexandria, Sydney, NSW 2015

This book was created and produced
for Franklin Watts by Ruth Nason

Project management: Ruth Nason
Design: Carole Bindin
Illustration: Jane Cradock-Watson
Photography: Peter Silver, Claire-Maria Cole
Consultants: Beverley Matthias/REACH
Resource Centre; Dr Philip Sawney;
William Sawney

Printed and bound in Belgium
ISBN 0 7496 4533 4 (pbk)

Dewey Decimal Classification 616.2

Acknowledgements
The author would like to thank all the
people featured in this book: in particular,
Darren Fairbairn, Michelle Newlove and
their families, Doris Hucklesby and William
Lambert. Also for their help and advice:
Alun Davies and Beryl Starkey.

The photographs on pages 4bl, 12, 15 and 16r
were taken by Peter Silver. The photograph
on page 13t was taken by Claire-Maria Cole.
Thanks are also expressed to the following
for their permission to reproduce
photographs: John Birdsall Photography,
pages 11t, 24r, 26l; Camera Press, page 25r;
Roy Castle Lung Cancer Foundation, page
25l; Format Photographers, pages 20, 21b;
Getty Images, pages 14b, 26r; Richard and
Sally Greenhill, pages 7r, 21t, 24l; Guzelian
Photography, page 27t; Photofusion, cover l
and page 16l; Popperfoto, page 6l; Science
Photo Library, pages 4t, 7l, 10, 11b, 13b, 17,
27; Truly Scrumptious, cover r; Western Mail
and South Wales Echo, page 14t.

Contents

Introduction

We begin to breathe from the moment we are born. We breathe air in and out, mostly without thinking.

Air is made up of several gases, including oxygen. Oxygen is the gas that humans need to live.

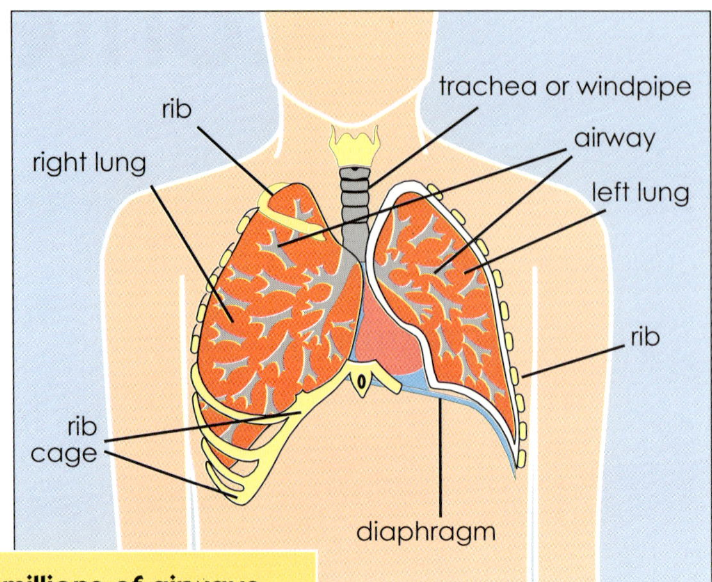

Making energy

When we breathe in, we take air into our lungs. Oxygen from the air passes into our blood.

Our blood carries the oxygen to all the cells that make up our bodies. In the cells, the oxygen reacts with sugar (made from the food we eat), to make energy.

Breaths per minute

Sitting down, we breathe in and out about 15 times per minute. Moving about, we breathe faster, because we need more oxygen to make more energy.

In a race, athletes like this speed skater take 50 or 60 breaths per minute. Their breathing soon returns to normal after the race.

The Kiss of Life

An accident, or a heart attack, may cause a person to stop breathing. Without help, he or she would die.

Using mouth-to-mouth resuscitation, another person can blow air into the injured person's lungs to help the person start to breathe again.

(Warning: NEVER do this to a person who is breathing properly.)

Breathing out

When oxygen and sugar make energy in our cells, waste is produced. The waste consists mostly of carbon dioxide and water. Our blood carries the waste back to our lungs and we get rid of it by breathing out.

Every breath you take

The way you breathe may express how you feel.
Do you sometimes gasp with surprise? Or sigh with relief? Have you heard people say they can 'breathe easily', meaning that they feel free from worry?

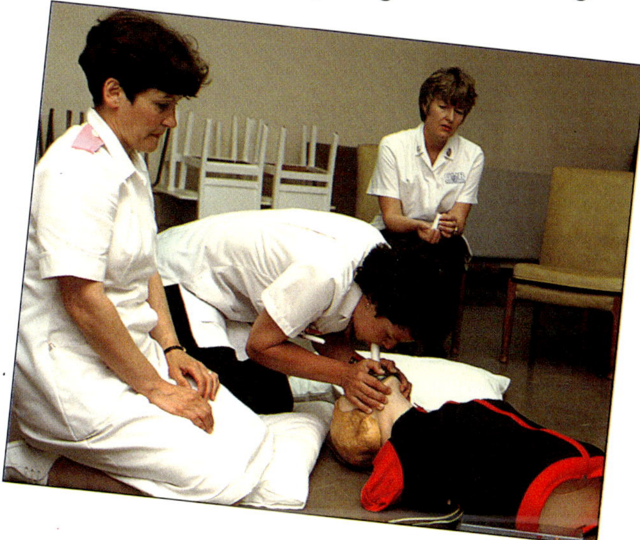

When people learn to give the kiss of life, they use a dummy.

About this book

In this book you will meet some people who have long-term problems with breathing. They can tell us why this happens and what it is like.

Think about breathing

Look at the scenes in these bubbles, and think about the ways people are breathing.

How many people in the pictures have learned to control their breathing for a special purpose?

How many people are wearing equipment to help them breathe?

Mountain air is fresh. But at high levels the air contains less oxygen than at lower levels. This is one reason why hill walkers and mountaineers become breathless.

You can learn to use your breath in special ways to sing or to play a wind instrument.

In outer space there is no air at all. A cord from the shuttle craft feeds air to this astronaut.

People may suffocate if their lungs become filled with smoke. Here, the victim of a fire is given oxygen through a mask. The firefighters wear breathing apparatus.

The fresh air at the seaside is especially helpful for people who have asthma.

This person is practising yoga, a technique for relaxing the mind and body. It involves controlled, slow breathing.

Being in the fresh air helps people feel fit and well.

Breathing problems

Do you, or does someone you know, have asthma?

It is a condition that affects the airways – the small tubes that carry air in and out of our lungs.

How our airways work

The lining of the airways is kept moist by a slimy substance called mucus. The mucus catches particles like dust from the air we breathe. It moves up the airways and we either swallow it or cough it up.

Pollen can irritate the airways.

An asthma attack
Two people described having an asthma attack:

'It feels as if I am being squashed.'

'It feels as if a rope is being tightened round my chest.'

A house-dust mite, magnified about 125 times. Every house has millions of these mites. Their droppings can trigger asthma.

Asthma

People with asthma have airways that are easily irritated. When this happens, mucus builds up inside the airways, and the surrounding muscles tighten. It is hard for air to pass through. The person begins to cough or wheeze, and may struggle for breath.

Things that irritate the airways and trigger asthma include pollen, furry or feathery pets, house-dust-mite droppings, cigarette smoke and traffic fumes. Cold air, having a cold, running, or eating certain foods may also bring on an attack.

Lung disease

Lung diseases make it hard to breathe. The main cause of lung disease today is smoking cigarettes. (See pages 24-25.)

Lung disease is also caused by substances that people meet at work. For example, coal-miners may develop lung disease from breathing in coal-dust. (See also pages 20-21.)

Air pollution

Fumes from vehicles, power stations and factories pollute the air. For some people, polluted air can cause difficulties with breathing.

▲ This worker is protected from breathing in wood dust.

Bronchitis

Bronchitis is a disease caused by germs attacking the airways and the lungs. The airways become swollen and infected. This makes the person cough and have trouble with breathing.

Cystic fibrosis

A small number of children are born with cystic fibrosis. The fluids in their bodies are thicker and stickier than normal. Mucus collects in their lungs and other organs, often making it hard to breathe – and eat.

As yet there is no cure for cystic fibrosis. People who have it must use medicines and do special exercises, to enable them to lead an active life.

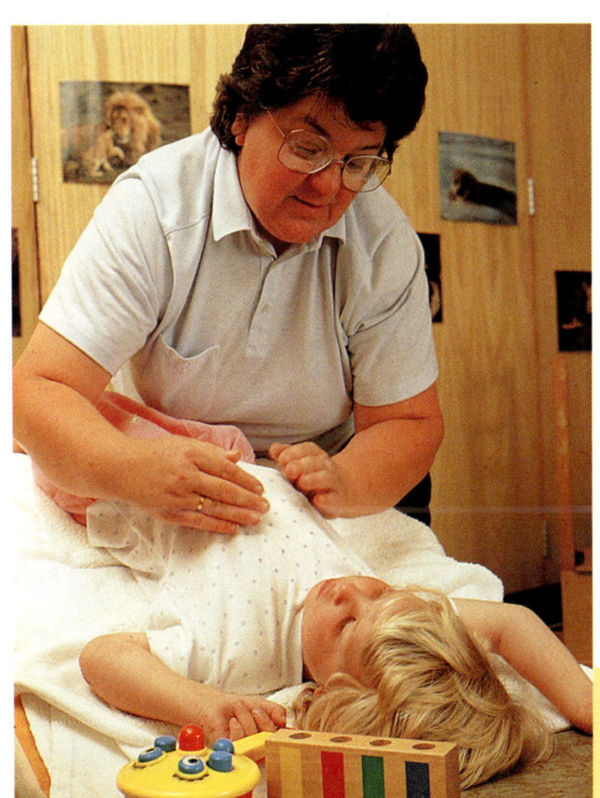

◀ This child has cystic fibrosis. Her chest must be slapped for some time each morning to loosen the mucus.

Meet some people
who have trouble with breathing

Darren Fairbairn

When Darren was little, he had bad asthma attacks. He often had to go to hospital.

Seeing him play football now, you might think he does not have asthma any more. But he does.

To control his asthma, Darren uses inhalers (see pages 16-17) to get medicines into his lungs. He uses a 'preventer' inhaler in the mornings. He keeps his 'reliever' inhaler with him all the time, to use if symptoms of an asthma attack begin.

If Darren catches a cold, it blocks his airways and makes the asthma worse. The chemicals in drinks like cherryade affect him in the same way.

Darren's parents think he has been better since the family moved away from London and its traffic fumes. They now live in a village in the country.

▼ Darren, 8, and his sister Danielle, aged 6.

Doris Hucklesby

Doris has three daughters, 12 grandchildren and 14 great-grandchildren!

She is a widow now, and lives alone – except for a lively budgie called Polly.

Doris has trouble with her breathing because of a condition that affects her heart. She has had this condition since she was a girl. The heart does not pump blood to and from the lungs as well as it should.

Nowadays Doris has such trouble with her breathing that she cannot walk far. Even talking makes her out of breath.

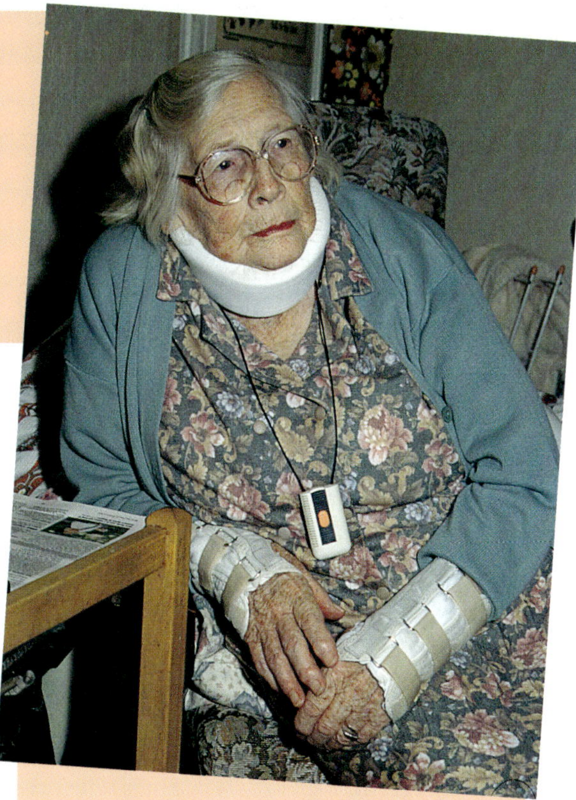

Doris has pain in her neck and wrists. A collar and strapping on her wrists help to relieve the pain.

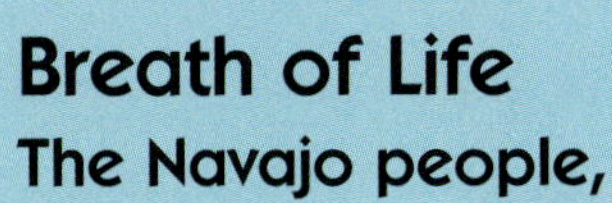

Breath of Life
The Navajo people, in the south-west of North America, believed that mysterious whirlwinds blew life into a person at birth.

They said that the patterns on a person's fingertips showed where the winds entered.

To increase the amount of oxygen getting into her blood, Doris uses bottled oxygen, which she breathes through a mask.

Lying flat makes it hard for Doris to breathe, so she sleeps propped up on pillows.

Her favourite time of the week is the day she goes to the Evergreen Club. She enjoys the company there, and she is good at winning the quizzes.

Meet William Lambert ...

William began work as a coal-miner when he was 14.

His first job was to load coal into the metal trucks. He says: 'In those days, ponies pulled the trucks. You could hardly see a thing down there. We worked eight hours a day, six days a week.

'The sandwiches we took for lunch got covered in coal dust, and we were covered in coal dust too.'

Later, William became a 'shot-firer', setting off explosions to loosen the coal. Then he was an 'overseer', testing for dangerous gas.

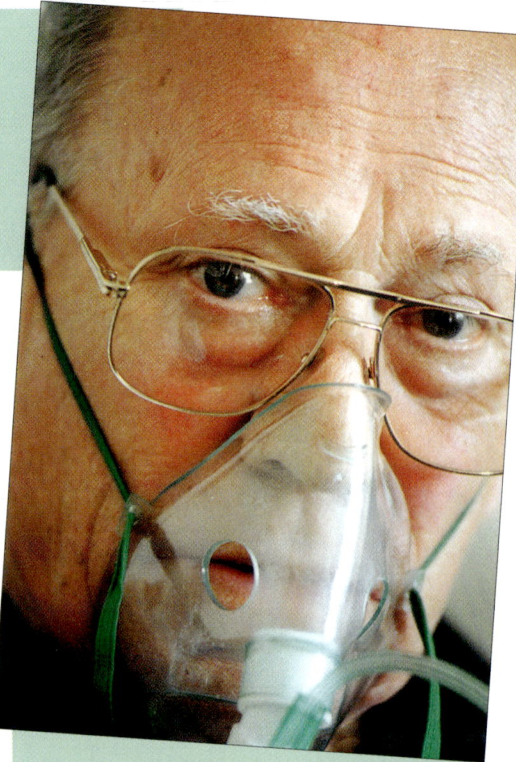

▲ Today William needs extra oxygen which he breathes through a mask.

Retirement

After 35 years, William stopped work. He became ill with pneumoconiosis, a lung disease caused by breathing in coal dust.

Now he finds breathing so hard that he cannot walk easily. He has a stair-lift at home, and a battery-charged scooter for going out.

William says he made sure that his sons did not go to work in the mines.

▼ A miner and a pit pony in 1934.

... and Michelle Newlove

Michelle, aged 16, won a National Achievers' Award for sick children.

She has cystic fibrosis. In spite of the difficulties she has with her health, she passed 8 GCSE exams.

The daily routine

Michelle has to be determined and organized every day. She gets up at 6.15 a.m. to prepare and take her medicines, using a nebulizer (see page 17).

▲ **Michelle with her mother.**

After breakfast, she lies on her special physio-bed and does exercises to help clear her lungs. Her mother slaps Michelle's chest and back to dislodge the mucus. Then Michelle uses her nebulizer and inhalers again.

At school, Michelle must eat at regular intervals, to keep up her energy. She may do more exercises at lunchtime. At night, she goes through the routine again: inhalers, nebulizer and exercise.

An active life

Even with this hard daily routine, Michelle used to do a paper round before school! Now she is studying Health and Social Care. She hopes to work with children.

▲ **Michelle supports Coventry City football team. She has a ticket to watch all their home games.**

Things that help

In Britain, more than three million people have asthma. That number includes one out of every seven children.

Asthma affects some people more severely than others. Some children with asthma appear to grow out of it. Some people only develop asthma as adults.

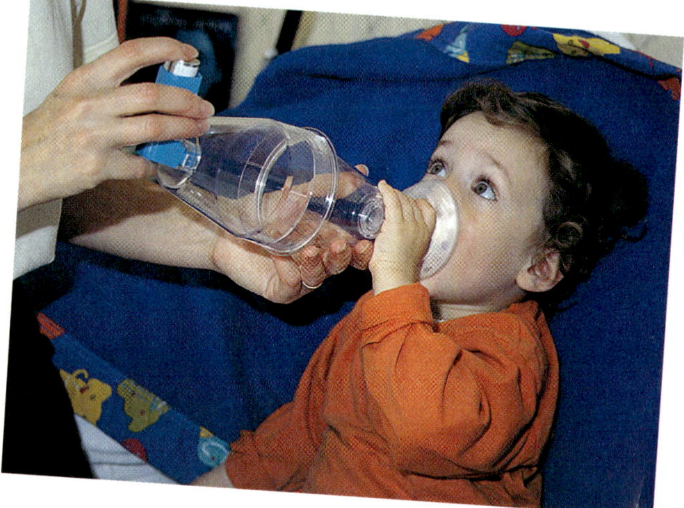

Inhalers

Many asthma medicines have to be breathed in ('inhaled') so that they reach the lungs.

These girls are using inhalers. The one on the right has a spray inhaler. She must breathe in at just the same time as she sprays the medicine into her mouth, so that it reaches her lungs.

The girl on the left has a turbohaler. It is easier to use, because the medicine is delivered as she breathes in.

Spacers

A spacer makes it easier for a young child to use a spray inhaler. It is made of two plastic halves that click together. The inhaler fits into a hole at one end. At the other end is a mask.

The medicine is sprayed into the spacer and the child can breathe it in, in his or her own time.

A peak-flow meter

Many people with asthma use a peak-flow meter. They blow one puff of air into it and it gives a measurement of how tight their airways are. It can help them decide if they need to use their inhaler.

◄ Using a peak-flow meter.

Preventers and relievers

'Preventer inhalers' contain medicine that helps to prevent an asthma attack from starting. They are used in the morning and at night.

'Reliever inhalers' are for when symptoms of asthma begin. They contain medicine which quickly relaxes the muscles around the airways. The airways open wider and it is easier to breathe again.

Nebulizers

People with severe asthma, cystic fibrosis and other conditions may use a machine called a nebulizer.

A small pump, usually powered by batteries, sends air through liquid medicine to make a mist. The mist is breathed in through a mask, as shown here.

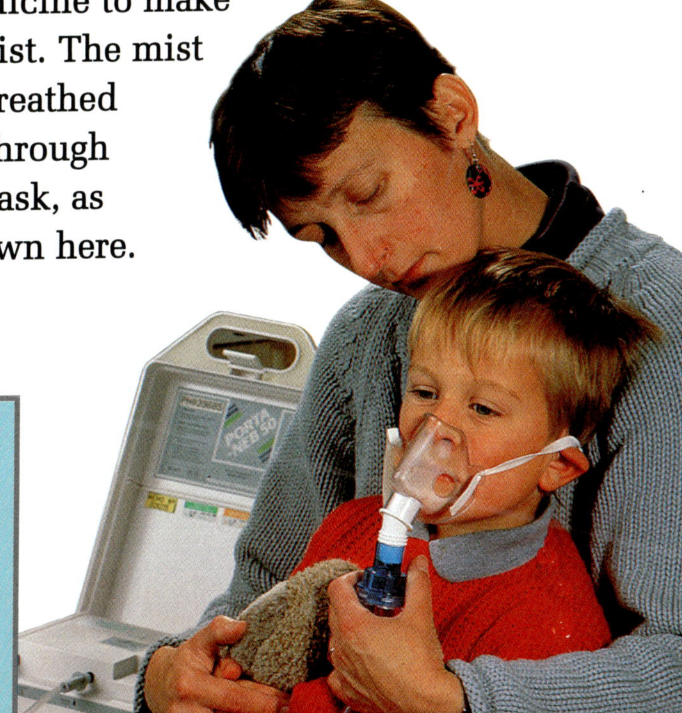

Understanding

If you have friends who have asthma, try to be understanding.

Perhaps they cannot visit your house if you have a cat or dog, or play in the park when pollen is in the air. But there are other places to meet and other games to play!

Living with asthma

A family is moving in to a house in the country. One of the children has asthma.

Some things that will help the child are labelled on blue boxes. Some things that could cause problems are labelled on orange boxes.

What other helpful and unhelpful things can you spot?

The house windows are shut to keep out pollen, but they can be opened to air the rooms. Damp and condensation cause mould to grow. Mould spores can trigger asthma.
Solar panels. These use sunshine to provide heating. There is no need to burn coal or gas, which cause air pollution.
Pillows and duvets filled with washable, synthetic material rather than feathers.
Breezy Cottage
Washable mattress cover to protect against dust mites.
Vinyl floor covering instead of fluffy carpet.
NO SMOKING IN OUR HOUSE PLEASE

At school and work

At school and at work people may come into contact with substances that irritate or harm their airways.

At school

Some things at school that could trigger an asthma attack are:

◆ classroom pets such as hamsters and guinea pigs
◆ fumes from science experiments, or from glue and paint
◆ certain foods, such as peanuts or eggs (for children with particular food allergies).

Teachers can remove some of these things, and children with asthma can avoid what they know is a problem.

Most children with asthma use their preventer medicine and take part in school activities just like everyone else.

Asthma triggers at work

Some people develop asthma
when they start work, in
industries such as baking,
farming and electronics, and
in jobs involving certain
materials. Things that may
cause asthma at work are:

◆ fumes from paint,
  glue, resins or chemicals
◆ dust from flour,
  grain and hay
◆ dust from insects,
  animals and wool
◆ dust from tea, beans
  and sawing wood.

▲ **Electronics workers in protective clothing.**

Health and safety rules

There are health and safety rules which
employers and workers must follow:
◆ Harmful substances must be eliminated.
◆ Workers must have as little contact as
  possible with irritant substances.
◆ Work-places must be clean and well-aired.
◆ Workers must be given protective clothing
  and must wear it correctly.

Danger at work

Breathing in coal dust has caused many
people who worked in coal-mines to develop
lung disease. Workers with some types of
asbestos (a material used for insulation) have
also developed lung disease. Some of these
people have been given compensation
(money) for the harm they suffered at work.

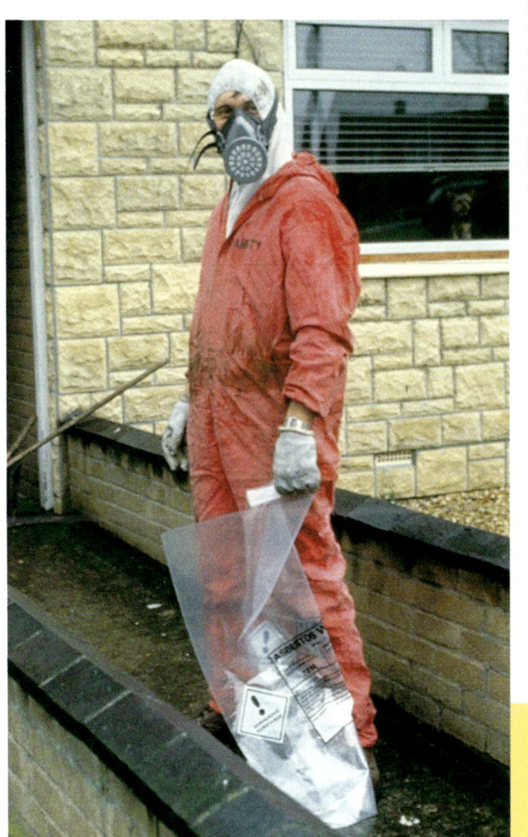

◄ **This worker wears breathing apparatus to
protect him as he removes asbestos
insulation from a house.**

The air we breathe

Look at the difference between an industrial town from 150 years ago (on this page) and a modern city (right).

In the past, factories, homes and trains all burned coal. Smoke from chimneys blackened the environment. Chest diseases such as bronchitis, tuberculosis and whooping cough were common.

Aeroplanes pollute the atmosphere.
Electricity and gas to light and heat buildings are produced by power stations which pollute the atmosphere.
Cigarette smoking is banned in most offices. These workers stand in the street to smoke.
This cyclist wears a mask as protection against pollution.
A modern city looks cleaner, but the air is still polluted – particularly by exhaust fumes. Some people blame air pollution for the increase in the number of people with asthma.
Pollution is particularly harmful to the growing lungs and tiny airways of small children.
Trees give out oxygen, and the park creates a 'breathing space', especially in summer.

The dangers of smoking

Doctors around the world warn that smoking cigarettes is bad for people's health.

People who smoke develop 'smokers' cough' and breathlessness.

Damage to the lungs

Smoke and tar from cigarettes damage the airways and cause them to produce a lot of sticky mucus. This makes it easier for germs to infect the airways and lungs, causing bronchitis (page 11).

Parts of a smoker's lungs may fail to work at all. This is called emphysema. Smokers also run a high risk of getting lung cancer and heart disease.

Harm to the whole body

Not just airways and lungs are harmed by smoking. Poisons in the smoke reach every part of the body.

A smoker's veins and arteries (the tubes carrying blood round the body) may be damaged so much that the blood cannot circulate properly. This can make it necessary to have a limb amputated.

This boy took part in a play which his class at school had made up, to persuade people not to smoke.

Passive smoking

A 'passive smoker' is someone who does not smoke but cannot avoid breathing in the cigarette smoke of other people.

Cigarettes can harm passive smokers. Scientists have shown that children whose parents smoke are more likely than other children to have colds, coughs, ear ache and asthma.

Stopping smoking

To try to stop the harm that smoking does, the government in Britain banned cigarette advertising in 1998.

Smoking is not allowed in most buses and trains, shops and offices.

However, cigarette companies make money from selling cigarettes and still encourage people to smoke.

Roy Castle (1932-94)

Roy was a well-loved British entertainer. He presented a children's TV programme called *Record Breakers*.

He was shocked to learn that he had lung cancer. Almost all lung cancer is caused by smoking – but Roy had never smoked. Earlier in his career, he had played the trumpet in crowded jazz clubs where many other people were smoking.

In the last months of his life, Roy publicized the dangers of smoking. He especially wanted his message to reach children.

Putting things right

Breathing in polluted air can harm our lungs. Over the years people have helped to put things right. But there is still much to do.

In London in 1952, this bus conductor carried a torch to show the driver the way through the smog.

A mask protects a cyclist from breathing in exhaust fumes.

Unleaded petrol

Exhaust fumes used to contain a lot of lead, which is especially dangerous to children's development.

People protested, calling for 'lead-free air', and from the late 1980s, unleaded (lead-free) petrol became more widely used. The government made it cheaper than leaded petrol.

An end to smogs

Coal-burning used to cause terrible smogs (smoky fogs) in London and other cities. The smoggy air made people ill with lung diseases like bronchitis.

In 1956 Parliament passed a Clean Air Act. It ruled that no-smoke zones could be set up. People were granted money to change their heating systems to use smokeless fuels instead of coal. Soon there were no more smogs.

June Hancock (1936-97)

As a girl, June lived near an asbestos factory. White asbestos fluff drifted through the streets, and children played 'snowballs' with it.

Years later, June became ill with a lung disease caused by breathing in asbestos. She wanted the factory owners to admit the harm they had caused. She took her case to the law courts and, in 1995, the judges agreed. They said that, even after the danger of asbestos had become well-known, the factory had harmed its neighbours and workers.

June was paid compensation for the harm done to her. Her story will help to make sure that health and safety rules at work are followed.

▶ **A photochemical smog over Los Angeles, in the USA.**

Photochemical smog

Photochemical smog is a new kind of smog that happens in cities today, in sunny weather. Sunlight reacts with pollution in the air. A haziness hangs over the city. People have a choking feeling, and their eyes water.

Most air pollution comes from cars and lorries, even though they are cleaner than before. We can all help by walking, cycling, or using buses and trains instead of cars.

Glossary

asbestos

fibrous mineral, mined from the earth. Because heat does not pass easily through it, asbestos was used for insulation and fire-proofing. Breathing in even a few fibres of some types of asbestos can cause lung disease.

asthma

a condition in which airways react to irritants, causing wheezing and difficulty with breathing.

condensation

droplets formed when water vapour (steam or breath) cools, for instance on windows in rooms where the vapour cannot escape.

cystic fibrosis

a condition affecting the glands that produce body fluids. It particularly affects the lungs and digestive system. In Britain about 5 babies a week are born with cystic fibrosis.

food allergies

Having an allergy or being 'allergic' to something means reacting badly to it. Some people are allergic to particular foods, such as nuts, shellfish and eggs. Eating the food causes their throat to swell and makes it hard to breathe.

house-dust mites

tiny creatures, invisible to the human eye, that live in beds, carpets, soft furnishings and soft toys. Household dust contains cast-off fragments of human and animal skin. The mites live off this. Their minute droppings can cause asthma and allergies.

irritant

a substance that can irritate the airways.

moulds

Moulds and fungus grow in damp places. They release tiny pollen-like spores which can harm lungs and airways.

physio

short for 'physiotherapy': the treatment of a condition by special exercises and massage.

pollen

tiny dust-like particles given off by certain trees, grasses, weeds and flowers.

rapeseed

a yellow crop used for oil and animal feed.

tuberculosis

an infectious lung disease. Most young people in Britain are vaccinated against it.

whooping cough

a serious illness once common among children. Most children now are vaccinated against it.

Useful information

ASH (Action on Smoking and Health)
16 Fitzhardinge Street,
London W1H 9PL
tel 0171 224 0743

The British Lung Foundation
78 Hatton Garden,
London EC1N 8JR
tel 0171 831 5831
(offers a free club and magazine, *Breathe Easy*.)

The Cystic Fibrosis Trust
11 London Road,
Bromley,
Kent BR1 1BY
tel 0181 464 7211
(provides support and information and funds research. A free Youthline on 0800 454 482 offers confidential advice to young people with CF and their brothers and sisters.)

National Asthma Campaign
Providence House,
Providence Place,
London N1 0NT
tel 0171 226 2260
(provides a wide range of information and support, including a School Pack, with advice on developing a school asthma policy.)

National Asthma Campaign Scotland,
21 Coates Crescent,
Edinburgh EH3 7AF
tel 0131 226 2544

REACH (National Resource Centre for Children with Reading Difficulties),
Wellington House,
Wellington Road,
Wokingham,
Berkshire RG40 2AG
tel 0118 989 1101

Roy Castle Lung Cancer Foundation
200 London Road,
Liverpool L3 9TA
tel 0151 794 8800

How to help

An asthma attack can be frightening – and dangerous. Follow these steps if someone has an asthma attack:

1. Make sure that he or she uses a reliever inhaler immediately.
2. Stay calm and listen to what he or she says. It is comforting to hold hands, but don't put your arm round the person, as this can make it harder to breathe.
3. Encourage the person to sit up, and to breathe slowly and deeply. Loosen any tight clothing, and offer a drink of water. (Warm water may be helpful.)

If the reliever does not work after five or ten minutes, or if the person is exhausted or distressed, seek help from an adult.

Index

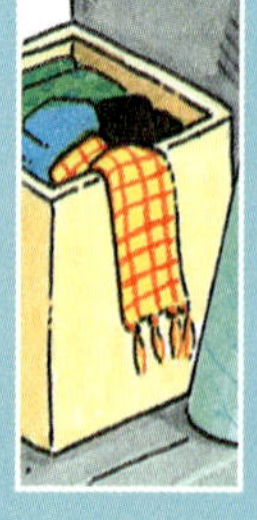

Keep warm
If you have asthma, wear a scarf over your nose and mouth on cold days. This helps you breathe in warm air, and keeps out the traffic fumes too.

Cold air and sudden changes of temperature can make you wheeze.